Endurance
for the
Journey

Bishop Jeff Poole

Endurance for the Journey

Copyright 2022 Jeff Poole

ISBN# 9798837345753

FZM PUBLISHING
P.O. Box 3707
Hickory, NC. 28603

Table of Contents

Day One

Resilience

To be a finisher, winner, millionaire, or even, a good man or woman, one must endure, and overcome, every obstacle until all goals have been accomplished. Training, or being physically fit, is not the key to finishing a long marathon; it is the mentality that enables a person to push through the pain while reaching for the finish line. The power of a strong mind, or resilience, is the ability to adjust to or recover readily from illness, adversity, or major life changes. It has been said, "life is not a sprint, it is a marathon." And because I have run in several marathons, I can say, this is a true statement. While running to the mailbox needs no mental power, running a marathon requires great resilience. I know, too well, the pain and power associated with running a twenty-six-mile marathon. In 2021, in order to run the New York City Marathon, I spent hours training and preparing my body to complete this type of run; this included building up muscle stamina through pacing myself. I also had to eat and sleep right, work out, then run. A big part of my training involved directing the internal dialogue of my mind so I could finish the race. It did not matter how hard I physically trained if I did not also spend time training my mind to be resilient which was necessary for my spirit, mind, and body. This mental training helped me to understand the importance of resilience and how to apply these strategies in life situations.

Throughout the course of a person's life, there are many struggles that take place within the mind. They can include marriage difficulties, medical issues, or even job situations that appear to have no end in sight. Because these situations can be long-lasting and unpleasant, one's internal dialogue can lean towards quitting rather than persevering. Though every struggle is different, the solution is the same. So, when it comes to marathons, I have had to fight overwhelming feelings telling me to quit; especially when my lungs were about to bust and my legs were screaming in pain. During those times, I had to silence those voices by changing my focus. It became necessary to anticipate markers throughout the marathon instead of listening to the pain in my body. In other words, stop signs, street lights, or the next opportunity for water became the focal points. These mental pictures were important in order to develop the resilience needed for me to cross the finish line. This can be accomplished in every life situation as well. Just giving yourself something pleasant to focus on, like a nice lunch, can ease the stress of a difficult work situation. Or, instead of focusing on all the debt owed, focus on one debt until it is paid off. With marriage, it could be focusing on date night rather than the challenges that pop up throughout the week. Resilience involves making mental adjustments in order to persevere through the adversities of life.

You were built to bounce back.

God put the ability, in man, to overcome adversity.

4

"But we have this treasure in earthen vessels, that the excellence of the power may be of God and not of us. We are hard pressed on every side, yet not crushed; we are perplexed, but not in despair; persecuted, but not forsaken; struck down but not destroyed." (2 Corinthians 4:7-9)

Therefore, it is important to remember, when the pressure seems too great and you feel on the verge of collapsing under the weight of the attacks and struggles, there is a greater power working within your spirit helping you to push back. Do not despair when you lack understanding of what is happening, we all deal with stressful situations. And, though it seems like people have given up on you, God never will. This is an unchangeable fact for, God says,

"I will never leave you nor forsake you." (Hebrews 13:5)

There will never be a crisis, or a situation, that He is not in the middle of it with you. However, we all fail in different situations. But what separates the winners from the losers is the ability to get back up and continue fighting for success. So, do not be afraid to make ADJUSTMENTS; BE FLEXIBLE AND ADAPTABLE. This defines RESILIENCE!

"Do not judge me by my success, judge me by how many times I fell down and got back up again" (Nelson Mandela)

Endurance for the Journey

Day Two

Never Negotiate with Doubt

Attempting anything new comes with risk. When people launch out to begin a new adventure, start a business, or move to a new city, doubt can creep in. Doubt causes them to fear then ask the question, *"What was I thinking?"* Unfortunately, before success is realized, they will first have to travel through the wilderness of doubt. It means to be uncertain about; consider questionable or unlikely; hesitate to believe. It means to fear or be apprehensive about; to be undecided in opinion or belief.

The strong, overwhelming feeling of doubt is the enemy to a person's faith. When those feelings attack, be assured, in most cases, this proves the Word of the Lord was heard in regards to starting something new, moving to a new place, or with any type of change. Feelings of uncertainty will cause a person to hesitate and not move; and, hesitation can be interpreted as disobedience. Therefore, before receiving a promise from God, it is vital to strengthen your faith. It will be necessary to build, within your mind, a strong sense of faith. This will silence any whisper of doubt that could creep in. Without this discipline, these whispers can cause people to negotiate, with the enemy, where their faith is concerned.

There are two kinds of people in every crowd, one who hears and, then, acts on the Word of God while the other negotiates his options. One night the disciples were in the middle of the Sea of Galilee with a storm bearing down on their boat. They were terrified of what appeared to be a ghost walking on the water, however, it was Jesus. Then, Peter heard the voice of the Lord say, "Come." As a result, his faith in Jesus caused him to act on that Word and he began walking on the water as well. However, the other disciples negotiated their options and stayed in the boat. One obeyed causing a Logos Word to materialize into a Rhema Word while the others neglected to work their faith.

"So, then faith comes by hearing, and hearing by the word of God!" (Romans 10:17)

When in moments of great testing, be very cautious of those who have been allowed to speak into your life. Be discerning of those who have been given access. Unfortunately, there are people who endeavor to prevent others from pursuing their Promise. And, it is here that most people find their purpose for life. Therefore, do not negotiate with doubt because it drains people of energy as well as focus. Speak the promises of God, out loud, in order to hear what is being said. Why? Because the Word is a powerful weapon that motivates and continues pushing people towards their end-goal.

When I signed up for the New York Marathon, I was confronted with "doubting" voices who had determined to talk me out of running. My age and the length of the training process (sixteen-weeks) were several arguments used to get me to quit.

But I came up with a Mantra, a repeated word, formula, or phrase that I believe helped. It stated, *"CAN'T QUIT-DON'T QUIT-WON'T QUIT!"* This enabled me to control my internal dialogue which was imperative to finishing the race. I believe it will also help anyone reading this. I would also quote scriptures like,

"I can do all things through Christ who strengthens me." (Philippians 4:13)

"No weapon formed against me shall prosper." (Isaiah 54:17)

For my situation, the weapons became self-doubt, pain, and mental questions regarding why I am doing this. However, they did not prosper.

Dr. Jerry Grillo gave me a formula for winning. It comes from the book of Genesis and entails: **1. Situation; 2. Reaction; 3. Instruction; 4. Warfare; and, 5. Reward.** Notice, the reward comes after the warfare. And, the warfare is to continue and obey the instructions. In other words, be deliberate in regards to your focus.

Another way to prevent doubt from derailing you is to keep renewing your mind.

"The average person has about 12,000 to 60,000 thoughts per day. Of those thousands, 80% were negative! And 95% were repetitive thoughts from the day before." (**The National Science Foundation**)

The Bible gives us a way to combat these statistics.

"And do not be conformed to this world, but be TRANSFORMED by the Renewing of your mind that you may prove what is that good and acceptable and perfect will of God!" (Romans 12:2)

To be transformed means to change in form, appearance, or structure; or, METAMORPHOSE. Think caterpillar turning into a butterfly. The question is, "how can people be transformed?" Fortunately, in this same passage, we are told, "by the RENEWING OF YOUR MIND." This means renovate, or a complete change for the better. To renovate the mind is to clean out all the old patterns of thought and bring in new ways of thinking.

Have I not commanded you? Be strong and courageous! Do not be terrified nor dismayed, for the Lord your God is with you wherever you go. (Joshua 1:9)

Day Three

Keep Doing What You Are Doing!

Upfront, I believe there are situations in people's lives that require changing, and adjusting, for them to work out for the good. However, I will explain what I mean when I say, **"KEEP DOING WHAT YOU ARE DOING."** Today's society lives in a culture that demands instant results. Some examples include losing ten-pounds in ten-days; five-steps to making a million dollars; and, retiring in twelve-months, at the age of thirty. Sadly, these only cultivate an attitude of instant gratification, however, nothing of value happens overnight.

It is great for those who happen to accomplish the instant results but, in most cases, people give up because it did not happen for them. Negativity is conceived and their internal dialogue tells them it will not work; then, they want to quit.

"Do not be deceived, God is not mocked; for whatever a man sows, that he will also reap...And let us not grow weary while doing good, for in DUE SEASON we shall reap if we do not faint." **(Galatians 6:7)**

God has established this principle as a law in the earth. So, if someone begins the process of working towards the fulfillment of their dream, it is vital to stay committed. As a result, progress will happen; and, out of a solid decision to win, it will come to pass.

Another principle states that the harvest is determined by the seed sown. Every farmer knows and exercises this principle; therefore, they plant seed according to the desired harvest. For corn, he plants corn seed; and, for tomatoes, tomato seed. The process includes determining the harvest prior to sowing the seed. It is silly to plant watermelon seed when the desired harvest is tomatoes. Therefore, it is necessary to work the principle of the seed for each type of seed produces after its own kind. And, once the seed is sown, the outcome is determined through a season of waiting. This is when it becomes crucial to stay committed to the process; because, after the seed is sown, the soil, sun, weather, and climate must do their job. This is a powerful truth; the seed is always in sync with the movement of the voice. However, if the seed is not placed in the soil, then the process of a continued cycle, of seasons, is missed.

The harvest process includes taking care of the soil because, doing nothing, is detrimental. It is also necessary to take care of the dream as well as the goals along the way to harvest season. This is the time to protect the seed by monitoring weed growth. It is vital to, immediately, pull the weeds in order to prevent choking the seed's potential. And, fertilizing the soil will keep it nutrient rich. Then, it is critical to water the soil so the seed will not die.

Regardless of your focus, whether health, finances, or relationships, "Keep doing what you have been doing." Keep going through the process and understand, though it may not be seen in the natural, what has been planted underground is working its way to the surface of the soil. I have discovered, by staying the course through the storms, trials, and adversities, the harvest will come. Though it may take months, or even years, the harvest promise will show up.

I can promise this, though it is not an instant reward, you will reap a harvest when you refuse to quit. Even after many failures, being committed to the harvest will bring it to pass.

Your Due Season is coming!!!!

"To everything there is a season." (Ecclesiastes 3:1)

As surely as there is a summer, winter, spring, and fall, this could be your season.

"Do not be so shortsighted that, if it does not happen right now, you are not going to be happy. You are sowing seeds that will reap a great harvest for generations to come." (Joel Osteen)

Endurance for the Journey

Day Four

Step Up

People have two choices when faced with opportunities to help, encourage, or inspire others. They will either **Stand By** or **Step Up**. Standing by, or being a spectator, never makes anyone great. But stepping up and stepping out will cause people to be remembered.

In the Bible, I love the story of Moses' courage and boldness while walking into the presence of the most powerful king in the known world.

"Moses went in and told Pharoah, thus says the Lord God of Israel: Let my people go!" (**Exodus 5:1**)

Up to this point, Moses had been standing by, watching sheep, on the backside of the wilderness. He did this for forty-years after being exiled, from Egypt, for a decision he made in anger. Though his motives were right, his reactions were not; he went too far by killing an Egyptian. After being exiled, he came to live in the province of Midian. This is where he became an insignificant person who served his father-in-law's family.

Many people currently feel insignificant and believe they will never make a difference. They have resigned themselves to "standing by" because they believe their opportunity has come and gone. Thankfully, today God is giving people another opportunity to **Step Up**. Despite their fears, failures, and wrong decisions of the past, He is giving them another opportunity to make a difference. It is still possible to be courageous and bold in certain areas of life. And, life is not over because of having a shady past. It is a fact; all people have a past and no one is flawless. Old or young, demographics excluded, all can Step Up. No one starts with big steps, they are small. What is important is getting up in order to step up.

When starting with health, it is important to STEP UP, then SET OUT into an exercise routine. Running a marathon is not the first goal, adding movement is. And, it is important to Step Up and drink more water and eat better foods; always with the goal of making healthier decisions.

STEP UP! In any marriage relationship, it is necessary to invest quality time into the spouse. A good way to do this is by scheduling a weekly date-night.

STEP UP! It is important to be actively involved in conversations. So, make a mental decision to look at the other person, or people, without adding distractions such as cell phones. Avoid being distracted by being in the moment.

STEP UP! Pay bills on time. Work on your credit score. And, start saving some money.

STEP UP! Be a giver. Put God first by being a tither; take the tenth off the top. Remember, tithing opens the windows of heaven enabling His, uncontainable, blessing to pour upon your house. And, just a reminder, the tithe does not belong to man, it belongs to God. So, by being faithful in bringing Him this divine portion, He will release His promises.

STEP UP! Start a retirement fund and develop a budget.

When Moses Stepped Up, the people of Israel were able to Step Out! They stepped out of four-hundred years of bondage, or slavery, to the Egyptians. Then, they walked into their promised land; one that flowed with milk and honey. By making an effort, their lives began a season of change.

Step up means to make an effort, to advance.

"Never underestimate the difference YOU can make in the lives of others."

This week, make an effort to Step forward, reach out, and help where needed.

Endurance for the Journey

Day Five

Awakened

Today, the challenge is to become AWAKENED. To be awake means to wake up, be aroused from sleep, be vigilant, and alert. So, to be awake is to know where you are in life as well as to know what you want to be and do.

I was inspired to write this during the sixteen-week training program established for the New York City Marathon. Every weekend we were instructed to add an additional two-miles to the run until twenty-two miles were accomplished. For this type of training, it was necessary to "arouse from sleep" very early in the morning. And a personal inventory was needed prior to starting a run; otherwise, runners could decline fast without completing the task at hand. Because it is hard to fix what cannot be seen, preparation is the greatest key for this type of run. Do not wait until in the middle of a run to fix an issue that should have been fixed prior to starting. So, be very focused and alert. Be aware of the surroundings and of the materials needed. Therefore, for the body, it is necessary to make an inventory of every item needed in order to complete a twenty-six-mile marathon. These are good instructions for everyday life as well. Most days are filled with personal challenges, financial decisions, various situations, and possible crises.

"Keep your heart with all diligence, for out of it spring the issues of life. Put away from you a deceitful mouth, and put perverse lips far from you. Let your eyes look straight ahead, and your eyelids look right before you. Ponder the path of your feet, and let all your ways be established." (Proverbs 4:23-27)

ATTIBUTES NECESSARY TO FINISH

1. **Guard Your Heart**
   When times get tough, or difficult, consistently inventory what is being allowed into your heart; especially regarding feelings and emotions. For whatever is based on feelings will ultimately fail. I experienced this many times as I began my exercise regimen. My feelings would scream, "WE DON'T FEEL LIKE DOING THIS! I'M NOT FEELING THIS TODAY!" At this point, it is good to scream back, "I'm doing this anyway." Then, it is important to practice faith mantras such as, "I am strong; I am more than a conqueror; and, I will overcome." Doing this will destroy any feeling that is getting in the way of the finish line.

   For out of the abundance of the heart his mouth speaks. (Luke 6:45)

2. **Control What Your Eyes See**
   While running, it is important to keep focused on the path ahead, otherwise, distractions could cause accidents. Remember, "Outlook Determines Outcome."

Keep looking towards the goal, stay on the path, and do not look back. And, especially, keep those eyes on Jesus.

3. *Keep a Guard Over Your Mouth*
During difficulties and trials, it is important to guard what is being said. The mouth can produce death or it can produce life. The Word of God is living and active, therefore, in the middle of hard times, speak His Word. By doing this, it activates life within those difficult situations. So, even when feelings scream, "Quit," His Word will increase you to another level of determination in order to stay the course. While running, I literally spoke His Word, out loud, when it got tough.

Death and life are in the power of the tongue, and those who love it will eat its fruit. (Proverbs 18:21)

For the word of God is living and active, and sharper than any two-edged sword. (Hebrews 4:12)

Faith comes by hearing and hearing by the Word of God. (Romans 10:17)

Be alert and do a daily inventory!

Pray this today: *"Search me, O God, and know my heart; Try me and know my anxieties; see if there is any wicked way in me, and lead me in the way everlasting."* (Psalm 139:23-24)

Endurance for the Journey

Day Six

Know Your Assignment

People should be completely convinced their life has a designed purpose and an assignment. They were not destined to only work a job, or have a career. And, I hate the statement, "to earn a living," because humans were not born for that purpose. Life is not earned, it is lived; and, it is lived out on many levels. People were designed with great purpose and they are here to fulfill a divine assignment. Assignment means a position of responsibility, post of duty, to which one is <u>appointed</u>.

"One of the two who heard John speak, and followed Him was Andrew, Simon Peter's brother. He FIRST found his own brother Simon, and said to him, 'We have found the Messiah [which is translated, the Christ]. And he brought him to Jesus..." **(John 1:40-42)**

Andrew believed his assignment, his duty, and his responsibility was to reach the people no one else could. What fueled his passion for the lost? Who, or what, influenced him to change? Who, or what, made such a difference? In the beginning, Andrew went to those closest to him with a story to tell. Just like Andrew, all people experience things that could encourage others. Just telling their stories can give hope in bad situations.

Andrew, the influencer, began talking to Simon who became one of Jesus' first disciples. Eventually, Simon was given a name change; Peter, which means stone or rock. He became one of the Lord's greatest leaders who impacted untold numbers of people and cities. Today, through social media, life stories are being told and they are helping people at the time they are needed. Part of my assignment is posting a one-minute post on Insta Graham and writing these devotions. As a result, people always tell me, "I needed what you shared." So, I challenge people to use their influence to help others as well. It could be that your assignment is to touch someone else's life with what God has given you to say.

"Before I formed you in the womb, I knew you; before you were born, I sanctified you; I ordained you a prophet to the nations." **(Jeremiah 1:5)**

Every living person was born with an assignment; a specific vocation or a mission in life. And, every assignment demands fulfillment. Therefore, no one person can be replaced nor can a life be repeated because every person is unique and irreplaceable in God's plan.

Task is unique as his specific opportunity to implement it. (Victor E. Frankl)

Day Seven

It Is Time to Thrive

It is time to ask yourself this question, "What kind of a mindset do I really have?"

"For as he thinks within himself, so he is." (Proverbs 23:7)

Therefore, whatever the mind conceives will cause the person to move in that direction.

"What is played in the mind will materialize in time..."
(Dr. Jerry A Grillo)

The Bible says that out of the abundance of the heart the mouth speaks. Thus, whatever proceeds from the mouth is an indicator of what is being played out in the mind. There are three types of people: 1) Those who are living for heaven, 2) those who are satisfied with surviving, and 3) those who desire to thrive. The ones looking for heaven only care about eternity while the ones who want to survive focus on paying their bills without losing anything. Finally, the ones who thrive want to live a life of overflow; they want to influence and help others. It is not possible for people to be a blessing if they only have enough for themselves. However, they are better equipped to do so when they are thriving. Do you find yourself thinking about what you do not have and how you are going to make it to the next payday? Are you constantly worrying about how you are going to pay your bills?

Today, I command lack to leave your mind and life! I speak over your mind and declare that you have a thriving mentality.

To thrive means *to prosper, be fortunate or successful, and to grow or develop vigorously. It means to flourish.*

At some point, most people have fallen into "survival mode." All have faced hardship, adversity, and misery in which a survival mentality was needed. However, if prosperity is the desired goal, this mentality must not be permanent. Moreover, it is important to learn from these hardships because they will become your story. Also, these are meant to make you stronger and wiser so what was once a mess becomes a message.

Hanani, one of my brothers, and some men from Judah came; and I asked them about the Jews who had escaped and had SURVIVED the captivity, and about Jerusalem. 3) And they said to me, "The remnant there in the province who SURVIVED the captivity are in great distress and disgrace, and the wall of Jerusalem is broken down and its gates have been burned with fire." (Nehemiah 1:2-3)

26

Notice, the Jews had survived their captivity, however, they were in "great distress and disgrace." They were not thriving. Remember, for those who are merely surviving, God's promise includes a future and a hope.

"For I know the thoughts that I think toward you, says the Lord, thoughts of peace and not of evil, to give you a future and a hope!" **(Jeremiah 29:11)**

God's gift of hope is the expectation that something good is going to happen. It is an anchor in the soul that steadies a person's life and keeps them grounded.

But his delight is in the Law of the Lord, and on His law, he Meditates day and night. 3) He will be like a tree planted by streams of water, which yields its fruit in its season, and its leaf does not wither; and in whatever he does, he prospers. **(Psalm 1:2-3)**

In order to thrive, it will be necessary to place your delight in the law of the Lord; He tells us to meditate, day and night, on His word. Why? Because that is the secret of prosperity. For in doing so, He tells us we will produce fruit and we will prosper. In other words, THRIVE!

Pray

- For renewing of strength to begin building again.

Yet those who wait for the Lord will gain new strength; they will mount up with wings like eagles, they will run and not get tired, they will walk and not become weary. **(Isaiah 40:31)**

- For the restoration of your soul (mind, will, and emotions).
  He restores my soul; He guides me in the paths of righteousness for the sake of His name. **(Psalm 23:3)**

- For the renewing of your mind and for your mind to be transformed.
  And do not be conformed to this world, but be transformed by the renewing of your mind, so that you may prove what the will of God is, that which is good and acceptable and perfect. **(Romans 12:2)**

- For the putting on of your new Self – for thriving.
  And have put on the new self, which is being renewed to a true knowledge according to the image of the One who created it – **(Colossians 3:10)**

"MY MISSION IN LIFE IS NOT MERELY TO SURVIVE, BUT TO THRIVE; AND TO DO SO WITH SOME PASSION, SOME COMPASSION, SOME HUMOR, AND SOME STYLE." **(MAYA ANGELOU)**

Day Eight

Endurance Decides Your Finish

"Success does not come from giving up!" (Thomas Edison)

Endurance is the ability to see past all failures for the purpose of seeing the finished work. Mr. Edison new this well because it took him ten-thousand attempts before getting the light bulb to work. When he made his nine thousand nine hundred and ninety-nineth attempt, he failed causing his assistant to react apologetically. However, he asked, "Why are you upset? Do you realize we are the only two people that know nine thousand nine hundred and ninety-nine ways of how not to make a light bulb?" He looked past the failure and saw the positive instead. And, without giving up, along with strong determination, he succeeded on the next attempt. He endured every failure until he accomplished his goal. Nevertheless, Mr. Edison had mental success before it became a reality in the present.

Are there areas in your life that have not been successful? Have you had plans fail and wonder how they will ever come together? It could be anything; maybe you wanted to start a business, or develop a healthier lifestyle. Maybe it was investing for your financial future, working on a stronger marriage, or having to raise your children by yourself.

"For you have need of endurance, so that when you have done the will of God, you may receive what was promised." **(Hebrews 10:36)**

In other words, endurance means constancy, steadfastness, and patience. This is a person who, amid great trial and suffering, is not swayed from his purpose or loyalty to his faith. One key to developing endurance involves forbidding the situation to affect who you are, or your purpose. It could be said that endurance is a form of character building.

"We also celebrate in our tribulations, knowing that tribulation brings about perseverance [Endurance]; 4) and perseverance, proven character; and proven character hope." **(Romans 5:3)**

Diana Nyad was a woman who best exemplified endurance; she refused to give up on her dream. She was determined to swim one-hundred and ten miles from Havana Cuba to Key West Florida; and, on her fifth attempt, she made history. September 9, 2013, without a shark cage, she swam the distance in fifty-three hours. All her prior attempts ended badly. Her first was at the age of twenty-eight and she did not make the second attempt until she was sixty-years old where an asthma attack pulled her from the water. The third attempt ended with being stung by Box jellyfish. She was stung all over her body and ninety percent of people stung by this jellyfish usually die. She was pulled out of her next attempt due to jellyfish as well. Though the past failures could have discouraged her from making another attempt, she did not let that stop her. She held on to her dream, refused to give up, and endured the difficulties as well as the challenges. Then, because she endured the struggles, she received what she had been determined to accomplish. Therefore, remember, after Enduring, you will receive the promise.

"I will not quit. I persevere and thrive in adversity. If knocked down, I will get back up. Every time. I am never out of the fight!" **(From the Navy Seal Creed)**

Endurance for the Journey

Day Nine

Unlimited

One simply amazing thing about life is how God created the human body with its capacity to learn and to grow. The word "capacity" gives the image of something large and means the power of receiving knowledge, mental ability, and maximum possible output. So, because we have been given not just life, but abundant life, we should rethink how we have been living this life. No matter what, we are here, and it is possible to live at a higher level with an unlimited life. Thankfully, we were not created to fail, nor to live in lack.

"Jesus came to give us life and a more abundant life..." (John 10:10)

"For You formed my inward parts; You covered me in my mother's womb. I will praise You for I am fearfully and wonderfully made..." (Psalm 139:13-14)

Again, I am amazed at the Unlimited capacity of the brain to learn and to grow. For this reason,

33

"Do not be conformed to this world, but be transformed by the renewing of your mind..." (Romans 12:2)

The systems of this world put limitations and boundaries on what people can achieve. But it is possible to accomplish more than what the courts, our backgrounds, any higher learning, or financial levels dictate. Neurologists say people have the capacity to hold two point five petabytes of information in our brains. So, what is a petabyte? It is one thousand twenty-four terabytes or a million gigabytes. A smart phone has from sixteen gigabytes to sixty-four gigabytes; or, one hundred twenty-eight gigabytes of memory capacity. For the brain, this translates to two point five million gigabytes of digital memory. This means the brain is capable of learning something new every second, every minute, and every hour of every day for a thousand lifetimes. So, never allow another person to put limitations on your life. It does not matter how young or old you are, or your station in life, "You are UNRESTRICTED!"

"The heart of the prudent acquires knowledge, and the ear of the wise seeks knowledge!" (Proverbs 18:15)

"A noble and God like character is not a thing of favor or chance, but is the natural result of continued effort in right thinking, the effect of long-cherished association with God-like thoughts." (James Allen, As a Man Thinketh)

Day Ten

The Ripple Effect

If you have ever been to a pond, or a lake, and thrown a rock into it, due to the splash it made, you can see its exact entry point. Then, as a result of the rock's impact with the water, a ripple effect was created that spread from its initial splash. People can also have that same impact on others. How they influence them can cause a ripple effect just as the rock did when it hit the water. Words and actions are like that rock, they can carry on, or spread, through many generations.

"For we are His workmanship created in Christ Jesus for good works, which God had prepared beforehand that we should walk in them." (Ephesians 2:10)

When God formed people in their mother's wombs, He did it with a purpose in mind. He specifically designed every human being with certain works to complete; and, He planned these works before the foundation of the world. Ruth is a good example of the ripple effect in the Old Testament.

Ruth made the decision to follow Naomi back to the land of Judah, from Moab, but did not realize the ripple effect it would have for generations to come. I believe leaving her country instead of staying comfortable, in Moab, was the beginning of the ripple effect. She enters a strange land just as the barley harvest was taking place.

And Ruth the Moabite said to Naomi, "Let me go to the fields and pick up the leftover grain behind anyone in whose eyes I find favor." Naomi said to her, "Go ahead, my daughter." 3) So she went out, entered a field and began to glean behind the harvesters. As it turns out, she was working in a field belonging to Boaz, who was from the clan of Elimelek. **(Ruth 2:2-3)**

Boaz was a wealthy relative of Naomi, Ruth's widowed mother-in-law. She found favor in his sight, and as her kinsmen redeemer, Boaz married her. As the ripple effect continues, she gave birth to a son named Obed. Now Obed was the father of Jesse who was the father of David. And through this line, JESUS WAS BORN. Ruth walked in the steps that God had ordained before the foundation of the world and, by doing so, opened the door for all humanity to be Saved. Be encouraged, though you might not see the on-going ripple effect taking place, your life is affecting many generations to come.

"I alone cannot change the world, but I can cast a stone across the waters to create many ripples." **(Mother Teresa)**

Day Eleven

Adapt and Evolve

Many people set goals for advancement, prosperity, or even getting in better physical condition. However, though the process looks one way in the beginning, it might look completely different as time goes by. The book of Joshua gives a great illustration of what adapting and evolving might look like along the journey.

After Moses led Israel through the wilderness and to the point of crossing over to the Promised Land, he dies. Joshua, along with the three to four-million Israelites who were expecting to enter another phase of their journey, must have been thinking, "Now What?" They were on the edge of a breakthrough and, now, there was a delay which stopped their progress. All the uncertainty must have overwhelmed them. However, in order to continue, all of Israel had to ADAPT. They had to be open minded and willing to adjust so this unplanned death would not stop the advancement of the fulfilling of God's promise to Israel. So, God commanded them,

"Arise, go over this Jordan." (Joshua 1:2-9)

For us, it is also necessary to take the next step. Obstacles will come but proceeding with forward momentum gives people a sense of purpose. Implementing the next step births a confidence in believing, "I didn't come this far just to quit." No matter the circumstance, adapt. Do not let the conditions of the economy, job layoffs, or even people leaving your life stop you from evolving into the expectations of success. It is okay, for the purpose of developing along the way, to move gradually. Just remember, the goal is to see the dream to its completion. And, Instant Transformation is not conducive to changing conditions.

"Be strong and of good courage; do not be afraid, nor be dismayed [depressed] for the Lord your God is with you wherever you go." (Joshua 1:9)

Know that God will never leave nor forsake you, therefore, obtain a new perspective regarding any problem or obstacle. Set your sights on the driving force behind the dream and get daily inspiration. Find a way to stay motivated and creative, then encourage yourself when the journey takes on a different appearance.

YOU WILL OVERCOME CHANGING CONDITIONS AND EVOLVE INTO THE PERSON GOD HAS CALLED YOU TO BE!

"You must be shapeless, formless, like water. When you pour water in a cup, it becomes the cup. When you pour water in a bottle, it becomes the bottle. When you pour water in a teapot,

it becomes the teapot. Water can drip and it can crush. Become like water my friend." (Bruce Lee)

Endurance for the Journey

Day Twelve

Do Not Compromise

When making goals, pursuing dreams, or making life changes it is important to avoid all temptations and peer pressure; either one of these can derail your progress. Temptations will arise to yield and compromise your standards and values; you must resist. To compromise means an endangering, especially of reputation. It is an exposure to danger and suspicion. Unfortunately, people tend to yield to compromise out of a fear of rejection, criticism, or feelings of missing out. Daniel was a man who would not compromise who he was no matter the circumstances. We can learn a lot from his story.

But Daniel made up his mind that he would not defile himself with the king's choice food or with the wine which he drank; so, he sought permission from the commander of the officials that he might not defile himself. **(Daniel 1:8)**

Daniel, a son of the people of Israel, was abducted and taken to a foreign land in order to be a servant in the king's palace. However, though he was in a foreign place, he "purposed" not to eat or drink of the king's delicacies. In other words, he made a commitment and was determined to follow through. Because Daniel's food standards were different than those in the palace, this resolve would be challenging to uphold. But, because he found favor and compassion with the overseer of the servants, he allowed Daniel to eat only vegetables and drink water.

"After ten-days, his appearance seemed better, and he was fatter than all the youths who had been eating the king's choice food." **(Daniel 1:15)**

And, due to him sticking to his commitment,

"God gave them knowledge and intelligence in every kind of literature and expertise; Daniel even understood all kinds of visions and dreams." **(Daniel 1:17)**

As God's people, we must also purpose, in our hearts, to not compromise our health, our mental health, our financial budgets, nor our relationship with Jesus. By doing this, when temptation arises, the line has already been drawn in the sand. So, to move forward, do not compromise integrity, discipline, or self-care. Be a person who keeps their word and whose actions match what they say. Make a plan and be consistent in the small things in order to grow larger. And take time to rest, exercise, and eat a healthy diet to have more energy. These are non-negotiables when attempting to reach any goal.

"Be careful not to compromise what you want most for what you want now!" (Zig Ziglar)

Endurance for the Journey

Day Thirteen

Yards After Contact

In football, "Yards After Contact," or YAC, represents how many yards are gained, by the running back, after being hit. So, why do some running backs go down after the initial hit, but others do not? In life, people take hits every day; they may take the form of divorce, loss of a loved one, or losing a job. No matter the form, there are keys that will enable you to take the hit while continuing to move forward in life.

Keep Your Legs Moving

"But those who wait on the Lord shall renew their strength; they shall mount up with wings like eagles, they shall RUN and not be weary, they shall WALK and not faint." **(Isaiah 40:31)**

Expectation in the Lord will cause people to be renewed, refreshed, and revived; it will keep the hits from preventing forward momentum. Our strength will be as the EAGLES, able to soar through the storms. And, weariness will not overtake us as we gain strength necessary to win. Finally, our walk will be in line with God's plan, enabling us to be powerful even when the hits keep coming.

Dress for the Battle

There is a dress code for every sports team; they also have equipment, when worn, that increases the person's ability to play as well as perform better. What if the running back did not dress properly for the football game? What if he neglected putting on his helmet, shoulder pads, thigh pads, or knee pads? After the first hit, he probably would not recover. Unfortunately, this is true for the Body of Christ as well. We are told in Ephesians to put on the whole armor of God. Why? So that we will be able to stand against all the schemes of the devil. By doing this daily, when the hits happen, we will continue moving forward and gaining ground for the kingdom of God.

Stand firm therefore, having belted your waist with truth, and having put on the breastplate of righteousness, 15) and having strapped on your feet the preparation of the gospel of peace; 16) in addition to all, taking up the shield of faith with which you will be able to extinguish all the flaming arrows of the evil one. 17) And take the helmet of salvation and the sword of the Spirit, which is the word of God. **(Ephesians 6:14-17)**

"It's not how hard you hit, but how many times you can get hit and keep moving forward." **(Rocky VI)**

Day Fourteen

Open Doors

"Open Doors" conjures up the image of access, or opportunities to walk into places one has never seen. It means *freedom of access*, opportunity given, and a recognized right of admittance. There are several types of doors: those you push, those that need keys to open, revolving doors, and doors that automatically open when you step in the right place. Sometimes it seems as though every door is closed, and locked; you have no key, no strength to push, and no idea where to place your foot.

"He who is holy, who is true, who has the KEY of David, who opens and no one will shut, and who shuts and no one opens, says this: 8) I know your deeds. Behold, I have put before you an open door which no one can shut..." (Revelation 3:7-8)

No matter the trial or adversity, God has given His people an open door that no man can close; and, for the purpose of protection, He shuts doors that no man can open. It is not the will of God for people to push through doors He has closed. And, when He opens a door of opportunity, it will come with resistance and battles because of the access being revealed.

"For a great and effective door has opened to me, and there are many adversaries." (1 Corinthians 16:9)

It is while facing these "many adversaries" that perseverance is needed. With it, going through times of opposition and resistance while maneuvering through an open door will bring greater influence and results. And, being able to be a blessing to others is one of the benefits of persevering. So, be encouraged, God has the key and He has set before His people an open door; therefore, it is time to enter in.

"When one door closes, another opens; but we often look so long and so regretfully upon the closed door that we do not see the one which has opened for us!" (Alexander Graham Bell)

Day Fifteen

Transition

Say it now! <u>I AM IN TRANSITION!</u>

I believe many who are reading this book are in some form of transition. It can take the shape of having a baby, moving to a new location, a child graduating from school, switching careers, or becoming empty nesters. Whatever form it takes, transition throws people a learning curve that must be navigated in order to grow without being stunted along the way. It means movement, passage, or change from one position, state, subject, or concept to another. Transition will always affect a person's emotions but will also affect how their life will move forward, or back.

As an example, the fans of the NBA Golden State Warriors, became very upset when the team moved sixteen miles to a new location. After thirty-years of being in the same place, they did not want to drive the extra distance to watch them play basketball. Their team had won two world championships and they had become very comfortable with the "original" home court. Therefore, the transition to a new one caused a season that included trials and storms along the way.

Another example, taken from the book of Mark, talks about the disciples being caught in a storm after Jesus told them to get in their boat and go, or transition, to the other side of the sea. Being in a storm is not a favorable position to be in, therefore, most people will turn around and return to what is comfortable. However, the disciples first reaction was to wake Jesus up. After He was awakened, Jesus preceded to rebuke the wind and the sea causing it to be perfectly calm.

It is also good to remember that Jesus is in the boat of life with all those who call upon His name. He is the peace Speaker who speaks Peace to every soul. So, do not turn back to the place of comfort but, instead, go to the other side. For no one knows who is on the other side in need of what God will provide through obedience. Remember, when the disciple's boat landed on the other side, the demon possessed man was waiting on Jesus.

THERE IS OPPORTUNITY IN THE TRANSITION. SOMEONE IN NEED IS WAITING FOR THE RIGHT PERSON TO SHOWUP IN ORDER FOR THEIR MIRACLE TO TAKE PLACE.

"If you already understand your purpose, are you prepared to change your plans to match God's will? If you are not, you can easily become bitter because things that used to work for you may no longer work. Be willing to transition at every stage of your life. If your heart is open and you have an open mind, the blessing will flow." **(TD Jake)**

Day Sixteen

Response Determines Results

With all the challenges the world encountered due to Covid-19, it was easy for people to become hopeless, depressed, and overwhelmed. The quarantines, job losses, political unrest, racial injustice, along with the mask and vaccine mandates caused them to believe their future was too dark to face. However, something good can come out of all the bad if the response is with a determined, creative, and focused approach. The power of a right response can bring about great results; look at Joseph's example in Genesis 37 through Genesis 50:20. Here are several principles taken from this story.

Joseph's Dream of Authority

Because Joseph had several purpose-driven dreams, his brothers became envious, jealous, and hateful towards him. They did not understand that God was preparing Joseph for a destiny that would preserve their family. Therefore, they threw him into a pit to die. However, he was captured and, then, sold into slavery. Though it must have been very confusing, Joseph was determined to stay faithful to God. And, as a result, God blessed and prospered him in all that he did. It is the same for everyone who will also place their trust in Him.

Even in Difficult Places, Keep Serving!

Joseph was falsely accused of rape and then thrown into prison. And, instead of screaming and yelling, "Injustice," he began to serve the guards as well as the prisoners. Therefore, as an example to follow, it is important for anyone in bad situations to do the same. Be a servant on the job, in your family, in your church, as well as the community you live in. Though it may not appear that changes are taking place, stay the course, "Change is on the way."

One Favored Moment Can Initiate Promotion

While Joseph was serving time in prison, the Pharoah's butler was arrested and thrown in jail. Then, while in prison, he had a dream. When Joseph heard about it, he interpreted the dream that enabled the butler to be restored to his position under Pharoah. However, the Butler neglected to inform anyone of what Joseph did. Then, after two-years, Pharoah had a dream that needed interpretation and the Butler remembered Joseph. Because God revealed the dream, Joseph went from being dressed in prison clothes to being dressed in Palace clothing.

Joseph's responses along with his determination to serve others during those difficult times determined the outcome of a severe famine. Then, after being reunited with his brothers, he showed great mercy to them. He said,

"But as for you, you meant evil against me; but God meant it for good..." (Genesis 50:20)

GOD WILL NOT FORGET YOU, HE WILL MOVE ON YOUR BEHALF. SO, KEEP BEING FAITHFUL AND LIVE WITH EXPECTATION!

Remember, when your responses are positive and activated by faith, great results will come. God will bring good out of every bad situation.

"Any man's life will be filled with constant and unexpected encouragement if he makes up his mind to do his level best each day." **Booker T. Washington**

Endurance for the Journey

Day Seventeen

Strength to Conceive

Today is not the day to be discouraged, it is a new day to remember previous accomplishments rather than reflecting on unmet goals. Therefore, because a new day brings a fresh start, do not receive the labels the world would put on you nor allow the negativity of others to dictate who you are or what you will become. Reject comments like, "You are too old, or too young. Or, you will not recover from this set back." However, pay attention to new ideas and release the dreams yet to be conceived. Hold on to faith and apply the strength necessary to bring forth the manifestation of what you are believing.

"Believe It, receive it… Doubt it, do without it!" **(Dr Jerry A Grillo)**

Abraham and Sarah, due to being ninety-nine and ninety, were well past the age of child bearing. However, God gave them strength in their old age to conceive.

"Through faith also Sara herself RECEIVED STRENGTH to CONCEIVE SEED and was delivered of a child when she was

PAST AGE, because she judged him faithful who had promised!" (Hebrews 11:11)

Keys To Birthing

1. *Sarah Received*!
   By faith, she took possession of the seed. Though, due to her age, it looked impossible that she could birth a child, she took Ownership of the Word of God. As a result, no one could talk her out of the promise because her future was a stake.

2. *Sarah had to Exercise Strength!*
   Because having a child was out of the realm of possibility for her, she had to exercise the power that resists doubt and unbelief.

3. *Conception of the Implanted Seed!*
   At this stage, development of the child has begun but it is not apparent to others. It is, therefore, necessary to feed your faith with the Word of God. Remind yourself of the promise, dream, or desire in order to remain faithful to it. Then, with encouragement, the promise will develop and begin revealing itself and have a great impact on others. It is Never too Late; Keep Believing!

Though I do not believe that a plant will spring up where no seed has been, I have great faith in a seed...Convince me that

you have a seed there, and I am prepared to expect Wonders!
(Henry David Thoreau)

Endurance for the Journey

Day Eighteen

No One Succeeds Alone

There are no lone rangers, therefore, I challenge you to make a phone call, send a text message, or an email to a person doing exactly what you would like to be doing. That person has already removed the rocks and paved the road and, most likely, would be willing to help you avoid the pitfalls they had to endure along the way. There is no point in doing it alone when there are tremendous resources available that will guide you into greater success. The, "I'LL JUST DO IT MYSELF," mentality is not from God; He created people to serve others.

Nehemiah had a passion, a burden, to rebuild the broken-down walls and gates surrounding Jerusalem. He traveled one-thousand miles, from Persia, in order to accomplish something that was much bigger than him. That kind of determination is necessary today. Through his determination, Nehemiah kept his passion alive by telling others of his vision as well as what he expected to accomplish. As a result, he was able to enlist people who could do what he was not skilled to do.

And I told them how the hand of my God had been favorable to me and about the king's words which he had spoken to me.

Then, they said, "Let's arise and build." So, they put their hands to the good work. **(Nehemiah 2:18)**

As an example, rather than running a marathon my own way, I enlisted a trainer who helped me gain strength and endurance as well as a massage therapist who kept my muscles from cramping. And, I received the nutrition advice necessary to keep my energy levels at a place I could finish the marathon. Nehemiah also understood it took a team to accomplish great things. Once the skilled people were in place, they had the wall and gates rebuilt in fifty-two days. It is amazing what people can do when they come together around a common cause. What would happen if we began enlisting the support, help, or skilled people who can do what we cannot ourselves? I imagine greater things; so, GO FOR IT!

Coming together is a beginning, staying together is progress, and working together is a success! **(Henry Ford)**

Day Nineteen

Do Not Go AWOL

The term ABSENT WITHOUT LEAVE, or AWOL, means absent from duty without official permission but with no intention of deserting. Therefore, no matter the excuse, it was required of them to show up. King David gives an example of going AWOL.

It happened in the spring of the year, at the time when kings go out to battle, that David sent Joab and his servants with him, and all Israel; and they destroyed the people of Ammon and besieged Rabbah. But David Remained at Jerusalem. (2 Samuel 11:1)

As king, it was David's responsibility to go into battle with his army, instead, he decided to stay home. What happens if we go AWOL from our jobs or our relationships? Though we are present in body, it is possible to be mentally and emotionally absent. The excuse of having a bad day or not liking a particular situation motivates some to checkout which can cause them to give their energy to other things. It is during these challenging times that fighting the good fight of faith is necessary. And, understand, people are depending on you, they are watching to see how you handle these difficult moments.

If we are faithless, He remains faithful; He cannot deny Himself. **(2 Timothy 2:13)**

Then it happened one evening that David arose from his bed and walked on the roof of the king's house. And from the roof he saw a woman bathing, and the woman was very beautiful to behold. **(2 Samuel 11:2)**

Notice, it goes from, "It happened," in verse one to, "Then it happened," in verse two. Being AWOL, David was in the wrong place at the wrong time. He should have been with his men, instead, he finds himself entwined amid a string of bad decisions. So, Do Not Go AWOL! Show-up to your assignment and watch what God does as a result of your faithfulness.

KEEP SHOWING UP! Quitting will not bring the results.

KEEP SHOWING UP! Do not make excuses.

KEEP SHOWING UP! Do not allow fear to stop you...be fearless.

Day Twenty

Hope

There is no greater power than HOPE; it is an expectation that tomorrow will be better than today. It is a spiritual weapon, a powerful force that enables a person to survive life's toughest challenges. This hope is provided in knowing that God Himself is the God of Hope.

***Now may the God of HOPE fill you with all joy and peace in believing, so that you will abound in Hope by the power of the Holy Spirit.* (Romans 15:13)**

Through the Word of God, the seed of Hope has been ingrafted into every believer's life. In every situation, hope makes it possible to recover the losses, regain momentum, and rise from every setback. During the battle, hope begins to stir and will activate a fight once thought gone. Job gives us a picture of hope when he thought all was lost; in one day, he lost his ten children; his income producing sheep, camels, oxen, and female donkeys; his servants; then, he suffered terrible boils from the soles of his feet to the crown of his head. However, Job lamented:

For there is hope for a tree: if it is cut down, it will sprout again, and its tender shoots will not fail. 8) If its roots grow old in the ground and its stump dies in the soil, 9) at the scent of water it will bud and put forth twigs like a sapling. (Job 14:7-9)

No matter what, just like the tree that comes back after being cut down, you can begin growing again. All it takes is the SCENT, FRAGRANCE, or AROMA of water. That small scent of water causes hope to explode; it can cause new growth to ignite out of every hopeless situation. For Job, this meant restoration of everything he lost. And, he was given double for his trouble.

Our human compassion binds us, the one to the other, not in pity or patronizingly, but as human beings who have learned how to turn our common suffering into Hope for the future! (**Nelson Mandela**)

Day Twenty-One

Delay is Not Denial

It does not matter whether a flight is delayed or the traffic is not cooperating, no one likes delays. Being out of control is not a comfortable feeling, therefore, the need to fix the problem overwhelms people. However, the good news, delays do not mean denial; they are set backs. It simply means, goals or dreams have been, temporarily, put on hold.

An example of goals being put on hold comes from the book of Numbers. It is the story of Joshua and Caleb spying out the land, of Canaan, with ten other leaders who were hand-picked by Moses. After spying out the land, they returned saying,

So, they reported to him and said, "We came into the land where you sent us, and it certainly does flow with milk and honey, and this is its fruit. 28) Nevertheless, the people who live in the land are strong, and the cities are fortified and very large. And indeed, we saw the descendants of Anak there! (Numbers 13:27-28)

Lesson One

There will always be resistance when attempting to advance any goal in life. With the spies, the resistance came from their own perspective; they saw themselves as grasshoppers compared to the giants.

Lesson Two

How you see yourself will be how others see you, therefore, see yourself as strong in God. See yourself appointed, anointed, and gifted to accomplish what God has given you to do.

Because the Israelites delayed entering the promised land, the people began to Complain. Then, excluding Joshua and Caleb, discouragement filled their camp. Because Caleb had a different spirit, and He fully followed God, he was able to enter the land with his descendants; he chose to rest in what God said He would do. You too can enter His rest; He will perform all that His Word has promised you and your family.

While Israel wandered in the desert for forty-years, everyone over twenty-years of age, who grumbled against God, died. Because Joshua and Caleb had patience, faith, focus, and a determination to continue living, they did not die. So, in a delayed season, do not complain, and do not give up too soon. Caleb comes to Joshua saying:

"And now the Lord has kept me alive as He said forty-five years, ever since the Lord spoke this word to Moses while Israel wandered in the wilderness; and now, here I am this day eighty-five years old. Yet I am as strong this day as on the day that Moses sent me; just as my strength was then, so now is my strength for war, both for going out and for coming in. Now

therefore, give me this mountain of which the Lord spoke..."
(Joshua 14:10-12)

Though there was a forty-year delay, Joshua and Caleb were not denied. By keeping your Faith, Focus, and Fight, you will not be denied either. You will see your God-given promises come to pass.

Remember,

> *JOSEPH WAITED THIRTEEN-YEARS*
> *ABRAHAM WAITED TWENTY-FIVE-YEARS*
> *MOSES WAITED FORTY-YEARS*
> *JESUS WAITED THIRTY-YEARS.*

IF GOD IS MAKING YOU WAIT, YOU ARE IN GOOD COMPANY!

Endurance for the Journey

Day Twenty-Two

Empty Places

With all the technology available today, the world seems crowded; it is as though the world is at our fingertips. We have access to increasing knowledge, all the information one can digest, and news programs all hours of the day and night. And, ordering products, clothes, or whatever can be done with the click of a button, then delivered within days. However, even with all this availability, people still feel empty. Fortunately, Jesus loves Empty places; and, the book of Luke provides an illustration of how Jesus took up residence in an empty boat.

So it was, as the multitude pressed about Him to hear the word of God, that He stood by the Lake of Gennesaret, 2) and saw two boats standing by the lake; but the fishermen had gone from them and were washing their nets. 3) Then He got into one of the boats, which was Simon's, and asked him to put out a little from the land. And He sat down and taught the multitudes from the boat. **(Luke 5:1-3)**

When Jesus climbs into the boat of your life, something is about to change. For this reason, do not get comfortable with empty; do not get stuck in a rut. In Luke, the fishermen were no longer fishing, they were washing their nets. They had fished all night and caught nothing so, at this point, they were done and had given up on catching anything.

Due to the enemy whispering his lies, people give up all the time; they try, but think they are too old, too young, too broke, or any other excuse, so they fail. Understand, because Jesus is in the boat, it is never too late to succeed. Having a relationship with Him drastically increases the odds of winning. And, a relationship is defined as *having a connection between persons by blood.*

When He had stopped speaking, He said to Simon, "Launch out into the deep and let down your nets for a catch." (Luke 5:4)

Jesus told Simon to, "Launch out into the deep." In this instance, launch meant to put the boat back in the water and go fishing. Simon was reluctant, tired, and hungry, but at His Word, he did what he was told. Jesus was not focused on Simon's previous attempt at catching fish, but on his obedience to the current instruction. Because he listened, Simon caught a multitude of fish. Today, it is important that we also listen to His Word for the purpose of obeying. Allow it to override any negative feeling and watch what happens in your life. What net could He fill for you? There are no limitations.

But Simon answered and said to Him, "Master, we have toiled all night and caught nothing; nevertheless, at Your word I will

let down the net." 6) And when they had done this, they caught a great number of fish, and their net was breaking. 7) So, they signaled to their partners in the other boat to come and help them. And they came and filled both the boats, so that they began to sink. (Luke 5:5-7)

As an example, at the age of nineteen-months, Helen Keller became deaf and blind, however, she did not allow that to stop her. As a matter of fact, she was the first deaf and blind person to earn a Bachelor of Arts degree. And, Nelson Mandela became the first President of South Africa at the age of seventy-six. Remember, there are NO LIMITATIONS.

Endurance for the Journey

Day Twenty-three

From Victim to Victorious

One of the most challenging things to overcome is a wrong perpetrated against you, or your family. By definition, a victim is one who has been subjected to oppression, hardship, or mistreatment; one who has been duped or tricked. These unfortunate moments can prevent people from moving forward and they can get stuck in the past. Complaining is a sign that a victim mentality has taken over. They begin saying things like, "If this had not happened, I would be successful." This statement can include being healed, or married, or any number of things.

When the ten spies gave a bad report in Numbers 13, after seeing the giants in the land, they declared they were as grasshoppers in their own sight. Words have power!

Death and life are in the power of the tongue, and those who love it will eat its fruit. (**Proverbs 18:21**)

As a result of this statement, Israel gave up and accepted defeat before there was ever a fight. Throughout the night they cried and complained against Moses and Aaron stating,

"If only we had died in the land of Egypt! Or if only we had died in this wilderness! Why has the Lord brought us to this land to fall by the sword, that our wives and children should become Victims? Would it not be better for us to return to Egypt? (Numbers 14:1-3)

Though they were complaining against God, His desire was to redeem Israel from their pain in order to provide them a Victorious testimony. However, the consequences of their complaining brought about the death of everyone twenty-years and older; they did not enter the promised land.

But your little ones, whom you said would be victims, I will bring in, and they shall know the land which you have despised. (Numbers 14:31)

Today, the cross of Jesus Christ has provided the Victory for all humankind. It is through the laying down of every hurt, along with sin, that burdens are lifted. Therefore, it is possible to pass out of a Victim mindset into a Victorious life!

But thanks be to God, who gives us the victory through our Lord Jesus Christ. (1 Corinthians 15:57)

"Defeat is a state of mind; No one is ever defeated until defeat has been accepted as a reality." (Bruce Lee)

Day Twenty-Four

Protect What You Have Birthed

According to the Small Business Administration, or SBA, ninety percent of small business startups fail within ten-years. Thus, when birthing a dream, it is necessary to have the right, knowledgeable people in place in order to keep the business thriving. In 1987, I started a church with approximately ten people; and, we met in a small trailer. In the first few years, I was told, "This will never work, you should close the doors now. No one wants to attend church in a trailer." Though it would have been easy to quit, we continued to thank God and refused to give up. It has been thirty-five years and, currently, the ministry sits on sixty-two acres of land with a 55,000 square foot church building. The people we minister to come from all walks of life and are of all ethnicities.

Moses was born at a time when the Pharoah of Egypt commanded all the male children to be thrown into the Nile River.

Pharoah commanded all his people, saying, "Every son who is born you shall cast into the river, and every daughter you shall save alive." (Exodus 1:22)

Because of this ruling, his mother hid him for three-months. However, it became impossible to continue hiding him so she placed him in a basket, insulated it, and placed him on the banks of the Nile. Soon, the daughter of Pharoah went to the river to take a bath; she found the basket and felt compassion for Moses. Afterwards, though she knew he was a Hebrew baby, he became her son.

In this story, the mother could not kill Moses because she saw that he was a beautiful child. And, for a business to become a success, it must be looked at as precious and beautiful as well. It is just as important for the business to be insulated from the negativity of others. Stay away from the negative things people think or say; avoid all doubt and negative self-talk; and, reject fear. Always build yourself up in your most holy faith, surround yourself with the right people, and keep praying so, "Nothing Can Leak into the Atmosphere That Would Cause Your Business to Sink."

Just like Moses was discovered by the right person, God can orchestrate the discovery of any business. And, because Moses still needed to be nursed, unknowingly, the Pharoah's daughter sent him straight back to his mother. Here Moses, his mother's dream, had everything he needed in order to grow and succeed. As you cover and insulate your business, God can send the right person to discover what you are building which can bring exponential growth lasting for generations. With Him, your dream will grow.

Every great dream begins with a dreamer. Always remember, you have within you the strength, the patience, and the passion to reach for the stars to change the world! (**Harriet Tubman**)

Day Twenty-Five

Keep Going When Things Get Tight

Years ago, my wife and I took our children to Ruby Falls and took an elevator, approximately, eleven-hundred feet below Lookout Mountain. Then, our guide walked us through narrow passages while we were navigating rocks and unstable terrain; it was a one-hour tour full of nervous moments. Life can sometimes maneuver people into tight places causing them to feel nervous and insecure as well. Instead of rocks, it could be financial, relational, or health issues that seem too monumental to overcome. However, after all the nervous moments, we came upon an awesome, cascading waterfall. After squeezing out of the last tight passage, it was an unforgettable sight as we completed the one-hour walk.

Many times, along the journey of life, this type of experience happens as we continue to press forward through uncertain times.

Brethren, I do not count myself to have apprehended; but one thing I do, forgetting those things which are behind and reaching forward to those things which are ahead, 14) I press toward the goal for the prize of the upward call of God in Christ Jesus. **(Philippians 3:13-14)**

Remember, we do not always know how it will look like on the other side of the problem, but it may be just as beautiful as that waterfall. So, keep pressing forward; keep pursuing; and, keep seeking after what lies ahead. Even though I experienced claustrophobia in those narrow passages, I kept going. Where necessary, I crawled and I would take one step at a time until I reached the place of reward. You can do the same.

KEEP PRESSING UNTIL YOU REACH WHAT IS WAITING ON THE OTHER SIDE – A WONDERFUL, AMAZING FUTURE!

"Believe you can and you're halfway there." **(Theodore Roosevelt)**

Twenty-Six

You Have a Treasure

Today's social media platforms enable people to see, mainly, the good stuff about a person's life; and, filters can make their life look even better. However, the outward appearance is shallow compared to the inward value God has placed on the inside of a person.

"But we have this TREASURE IN EARTHEN VESSELS, that the excellence of the power may be of God and not of us." **(2 Corinthians 4:7)**

Treasure is wealth or riches stored or accumulated; it is wealth, rich materials, or valuable things; and, it is anything or person greatly valued or highly prized. God has stored good things inside what He calls, "Earthen vessels." An earthen container, or object, is made of clay that is baked so that it becomes hard. God made man as an earthen vessel where He imparted gifts, talents, hope, peace, joy, love, light, etc. As a fragile piece of clay, man goes through tough times, endures life's pressures, feels confused about what is happening around them as well as lacks understanding of the troubles in the world.

Remember this when you are knocked down by trouble or are being persecuted for believing in the Lord Jesus Christ.

"We are hard pressed on every side, yet not crushed; we are perplexed, but not in despair; persecuted, but not forsaken, struck down, but not destroyed." **(2 Corinthians 4:8-9)**

According to this scripture, there is Hope and recovery for every situation; NOT CRUSHED-NOT IN DESPAIR-NOT FORSAKEN-NOT DESTROYED! As a result of His deposited treasure, no matter what comes against the person, there is still purpose and destiny. Therefore, God will be seen and others will be encouraged to keep moving forward. His power will move through the person without having to apply a filter.

"...look, as the clay is in the potter's hand so are you in my hand..." **(Jeremiah 18:6)**

Stay on the wheel for God is still molding and shaping every EARTHEN VESSEL!

"God never loses sight of the treasure which He has placed in our earthen vessels." **(Charles Haddon Spurgeon)**

Day Twenty-Seven

Work Your Land

Many people think, "If I had more money, better opportunities, a bigger business, more education, or a better background I could accomplish much more." These excuses defy the fact that every need has already been met.

"He who works HIS LAND will be satisfied with bread, but he who follows vain things is devoid of understanding." **(Proverbs 12:11)**

Notice, it says, "Work Your Land." It does not say working someone else's land. Start where you are and use your available resources.

Plow Your Ground

My family owned a one-acre lot and every spring they would plant a huge garden. They would prepare, or plow, the ground for the seed, otherwise, it would not produce. Then, they planted the seed, kept the weeds from choking the plants, and waited for the harvest. In other words, they worked the land. So, when you have a dream, a destiny, and a purpose do not wait for a better job, work your job to the best of your ability; do not wait to invest for the future, start small and start today; start a workout plan so you can lose those extra pounds; in order to know God, read a scripture per day until your hunger increases; and, start praying until you can pray longer than a five-minute prayer. Just Work the Land and the harvest will come.

Water the Seed

It is vital to keep the seed watered. Water helps to transport nutrients from the soil into the plant's cell structure. Therefore, it is important to water your dreams as well. This is done by speaking the Word of life over them; the life in His word gives viability to your dreams. And, the water of the Word nurtures the soil of your heart with Faith. It also helps to surround yourself with people who can keep you accountable to the seed you have planted. All of this together, with prayer, causes life to be transported into the heart of a person.

Harvest

For those who have worked their land, harvest is coming!

"While the earth remains, seedtime and harvest, cold and heat, winter and summer, and day and night shall not cease." **(Genesis 8:22)**

Do not be deceived, God is not mocked; for whatever a man sows, that he will also reap. 8) For he who sows to his flesh will of the flesh reap corruption, but he who sows to the Spirit will of the Spirit reap everlasting life. 9) And let us not grow weary while doing good, for in due season we shall reap if we do not lose heart. (Galatians 6:7-9)

PLOW THE GROUND-WATER IT-THE HARVEST WILL COME!

Do not judge each day by the harvest you reap but by the seeds you plant! – (Robert Louis Stevenson)

Endurance for the Journey

Day Twenty-Eight

Get Up

Trauma can be a major setback for people; it causes them to get stuck so their life never moves forward. Thankfully, today can be the day you GET UP and begin moving again. In the bible, Jesus encountered many of these people as He journeyed from place to place.

In these (five porches at Bethesda) lay a great multitude of sick people, blind, lame, paralyzed, waiting for the moving of the water. 4) For an angel went down at a certain time into the pool and stirred up the water; then whoever stepped in first, after the stirring of the water, was made well of whatever disease he had. 5) Now a certain man was there who had an infirmity thirty-eight years. 6) When Jesus saw him lying there, and knew that he already had been in that condition a long time, He said to him, "Do you want to be made well?" **(John 5:3-6)**

Notice, he was lying around other people who were just as sick, or sicker, than him; this probably had a detrimental effect upon him. It is important to surround yourself with people who can help push you towards your dreams rather than those who have given up on theirs. However, Jesus asked him, "Do you want to be made well?" then, everything changed. That is a question everyone should ask of themselves.

The sick man answered Him, "Sir, I have no man to put me into the pool when the water is stirred up; but while I am coming, another steps down before me." 8) Jesus said to him, "Rise, take up your bed and walk." 9) And immediately the man was made well, took up his bed, and walked. (John 5:7-9)

It is crucial to motivate yourself instead of blaming others for what you have not been able to accomplish. It is time to Get Up! Jesus does not acknowledge excuses; He gives the command and we are to obey. In his obedience, the man was made well. Thus, after getting up, momentum will keep you moving forward. As a result, being stuck will never be an option again.

If life knocks you down, try to land on your back. Because if you can look up, you can get up. And if you get up, you can stand up, you can fight for your dream once again. You have GREATNESS within you! (Les Brown)

Day Twenty-Nine

Power of Perspective

Perspective is a point of view; it is an attitude toward or a way of regarding something. Not everyone has the same point of view. Going through life's trials can produce either a negative perspective, or a positive one; a person's belief system will determine if it will be positive. Through Jesus Christ, our faith in God can develop a positive perspective.

And we know that all things work together for good to those who love God, to those who are the called according to His purpose. (**Romans 8:28**)

In general, all people get depressed, or feel discouraged, about the struggles they face.

Yet in all these things we are more than conquerors through Him who loved us. (**Romans 8:37**)

It is even possible to have a positive perspective when other people have wronged you. In the Bible, Joseph had plenty of opportunity to develop a wrong perspective. His brothers threw him into a pit to die, he was sold into slavery, then, he was thrown into a dungeon after falsely accused of rape. However, when he finally met his brothers again, his response was:

Joseph said to them (his brothers), "Do not be afraid, for am I in the place of God? 20) But as for you, you meant evil against me; but God meant it for good, in order to bring it about as it is this day, to save many people alive. **(Genesis 50:19-20)**

Though you may be going through a dark, valley experience, you do not have to give up. You can be like David, who said,

Yea, though I walk through the valley of the shadow of death, I will fear no evil; for You are with me; Your rod and Your staff, they comfort me. 5) You prepare a table before me in the presence of my enemies; You anoint my head with oil; my cup runs over. **(Psalm 23:4-5)**

In other words, God has already Prepared everything we would need to make it to the other side. Keep Walking! Though the way may be unclear, our hope and future are in God.

For I know the thoughts that I think toward you, says the LORD, thoughts of peace and not of evil, to <u>give you a future and a hope.</u>

Remember, perspective is an attitude toward, or one's point of view. And, remember to keep your faith, your belief system, in God, then good things will come.

Keep your thoughts positive because they will become your words. Keep your words positive because they will become your behavior. Keep your behavior positive because it will become your habits. Keep your habits positive because they will become your values. Keep your values positive because they will become your destiny! **(Mahatma Gandhi)**

Endurance for the Journey

Day Thirty

A Position Shift

Most people desire a better future than the past they survived; or, a better position in life. This is what happens when people become believers in the Lord Jesus Christ.

He has delivered us from the power of darkness and conveyed us into the kingdom of the Son of His love... (Colossians 1:13)

But you are a chosen generation, a royal priesthood, a holy nation, His own special people, that you may proclaim the praises of Him who called you out of darkness into His marvelous light; 10) who once were not a people but are now the people of God, who had not obtained mercy but now have obtained mercy. (1 Peter 2:9-10)

This is what I call, "POSITION SHIFT IN LIFE!" Shift means to change direction, transfer, out maneuver, to exchange, and to move from one person to another. It does not matter a person's current position; however, a believer's rightful place is in walking, living, and knowing their rights in the Kingdom of God. King David was a perfect illustration of this.

Now David said, "Is there still anyone who is left of the house of Saul, that I may show him kindness for Jonathan's sake?" (2 Samuel 9:1)

Jonathan was a close friend of David; and, when Saul was attempting to kill David, he helped him escape. Therefore, years later, King David remembered his promise to take care of Jonathan's family. This is a picture of God who always works to show kindness to His children. As a result of David's question, one of Jonathan's sons, Mephibosheth, who was lame in his feet, was instated to his rightful place at the King's table. However, prior to this, he was living in a wilderness place called, "Lo Debar." He needed a POSITION SHIFT!

Notice, everyone identified him as, "The one with lame feet." Sadly, people identify others by their weaknesses, failures, and disabilities. They say things like, "there goes the drunk, the addict, or the one who filed for bankruptcy." Or, "that's the divorcee, or loser." These are all terms that define a person's past; BUT A PERSON'S PAST DOES NOT DISQUALIFY THEM FOR THEIR NEXT POSITION.

When Mephibosheth was brought into the presence of the king, he devalued himself by saying,

"Then he bowed himself, and said, 'What is your servant, that you should look upon such a dead dog as I?'" (2 Samuel 9:8)

Because God looks at people as winners, overcomers, and conquerors, they should never present themselves as having no value. Remember, you have been forgiven, delivered, and healed, and your Position Shift qualifies you to eat at God's table. Mephibosheth also had a Position Shift which qualified him to eat at King David's table.

But Mephibosheth your master's son shall eat bread at my table always. **(2 Samuel 9:10)**

Receive your POSITION SHIFT TODAY! KNOW THAT GOD HAS YOU!

God will not allow any person to keep you from your destiny. They may be bigger, stronger, or more powerful, but God knows how to shift things around and get you to where you are supposed to be! **(Joel Osteen)**

Endurance for the Journey

Day Thirty-One

Walk This Way

Even as you have walked this journey through many places, encountering all sorts of experiences, do not get comfortable. Do Not Get Stuck! For God has a multitude of new places He would have you walk. However, it will take trusting Him to lead you along the path He has chosen.

In the book of Joshua there were over two-million people waiting to cross over the Jordan River. It was the promise of entering a land flowing with milk and honey that brought them to this place. The land would provide greater opportunities, new territories, and new connections; however, it would take walking in places they had never seen before.

"When you see the ark of the covenant of the Lord your God, and the priests, the Levites, bearing it, then you shall <u>set out from your place</u> and go after it. (Joshua 3:3)

SET OUT FROM YOUR PLACE meant to leave a place and begin a journey; imagine their anticipation and excitement along with their uncertainty. Though the destination was unseen, every step meant a new experience.

For we walk by faith, not by sight. **(2 Corinthians 5:7)**

Everyone's place is different; one person's place could be starting a new business while someone else's could be moving to a new city. Whatever THE PLACE, it is time to take the first step. For me, my journey into the new, and uncertain, began with joining the Air Force, getting married, and moving six-hundred miles from home; all at the age of nineteen. Then, I started Pastoring a church, was involved in three building projects, and I ran three marathons.

And Joshua said to the people, "Sanctify yourselves, for tomorrow the Lord will do wonders among you." (Joshua 3:5)

Be encouraged, as you begin to walk toward the NEW, God will do His part. So, do not turn back but continue moving into the unfamiliar. It is here that God will reveal things you never knew about yourself and things you never knew you could do.

...For you have not passed this way before.

So, I say, "Go for it!" WALK THIS WAY!

The Only Impossible Journey is the one you never begin! **(Tony Robbins)**